Cosy Burrow Books

VALKYRIE ACADEMY DRAGON ALLIANCE
Book Two

VANISHED

I0585605

"*As a wingless Valkyrie, Kara strives not only for her own importance on Asgard but fights for justice for all creatures, even creatures that spout fire. This fast-paced read will inspire readers to fight for justice and maybe even acquire their very own dragon.*" *Jessie B., Proofreader, Red Adept Editing*

VALKYRIE ACADEMY DRAGON ALLIANCE BOOKS

Cosy Burrow Books

VALKYRIE ACADEMY DRAGON ALLIANCE

VANISHED

KATRINA COPE

My family ~ For your never-ending support

GET UPDATES & NOTIFICATIONS OF GIVEAWAYS

Would you like a FREE copy of Marked?
Visit here:

https://www.katrinacopebooks.com/valkyrie-academy-dragon-alliance

Through this link you can sign up for my newsletter and receive a FREE copy of Marked plus updates about my fantasy books, sales and notification of giveaways.

- CHAPTER ONE -

Sitting on the edge of my bed, I wait with a churning stomach. If Elan is right, Odin is about to storm through my door. Hildr's squeaking leather pants don't ease my tension as she paces the room. I gaze at Eir. Even the calm one is sitting on the edge of her seat and fiddling with her fingers.

The door swings open, and Mistress Sigrun storms into the room. Her face is long, showing off her picture-perfect beauty, yet the expression on her face portrays something to be feared. In her annoyance, she has stretched out her majestic white wings, making her appear more intimidating.

Odin brushes her wing aside and pushes past her. Elan was right. He looks irate. His eye not covered by a patch glares at me with the look that he gave me not that long ago when Heimdall dragged me to his palace. I don't understand what I've done wrong. If anything, he should be thanking me for Elan's and my assistance in saving the winged Valkyries and our academy from danger. We saved the day. *Doesn't that at least deserve a smile and thanks?*

He stomps farther into the room and stands in the center. His eye bulges as he glares at each one of us individually. I didn't know that Odin did house calls. He must be furious over something.

Hildr abruptly stops pacing and stands still in the middle of the room, not far from Odin.

Odin's eye rests directly on me. A lump forms in my throat, restricting my airflow. I attempt to swallow and struggle to move the lump an inch.

Odin places his hands on his hips, and his red cloak drapes gracefully over his elbows, making him appear broader and more intimidating. He tilts his jaw higher and glares at me. "Young Valkyrie, of the wingless kind. Mistress Sigrun has informed me that you have refused to hand over your dragon."

My jaw drops as I stare at him, dumbfounded. We have just protected Asgard, and this is how he treats us. I thought he would be thrilled with our efforts and would be rewarding us. Despite feeling intimidated, I straighten my shoulders and look him square in the face. "Yes. I believe she deserves to remain free. She helped save us where the winged Valkyries failed. I think that letting her remain free is the least that we can do to thank her. After all, she did come of her own free will. She is not one of the sacrificial dragon young."

His glower deepens. "The dragons have made an alliance with us. They must give us one of their young dragons. The Valkyries and our warriors need to practice their fighting skills against such beasts in case any of them decide to turn against us. And this dragon is an emperor dragon. We do not have any of them. They have not honored the alliance by giving us one of them." He moves to tower over me.

Holding my ground, I broaden my shoulders farther. "It is my understanding that the emperor dragons are not required to hand over one of their young because they are a rare kind, and their existence is endangered." I can't help raising my chin as I say this. Though I regard Odin with all the respect he is due, I can't stand this injustice.

"Did you not say that the nest you saved this egg from consisted of three eggs?" Odin's eyebrow lifts as he gazes down at me.

I don't know how he knows, but clearly, someone has told him my story. "Yes. I did. This was a couple of years ago."

He has a twinkle in his eye as though he thinks that he has outsmarted me. "Three eggs are a large amount for a dragon to have in one batch. This would make it evident that these dragons are not endangered anymore. So now, they must honor their agreement and hand over a young one every year."

My mouth falls open. "I don't know if these other two eggs survived and hatched. I have not asked."

Odin chuckles. "*Asked.* You act as though they can speak to you."

"I-I-I guess I mean that I haven't asked the other Valkyries if they have seen the three babies." I curse myself for my mistake. It has become clear that they don't know that I can speak to the dragons and that the dragons are capable of speaking to us. A thought runs through my head, and I frown. "How did you make a treaty if you can't speak to the dragons? There must be some way you can communicate with them to form an agreement."

Odin puffs out his chest and starts to pace the room. "An emperor dragon made the agreement many years ago. Loki managed to shape-shift into a dragon form, and he then communicated with the dragons, and this is how the alliance was agreed upon."

"Loki can shape-shift into a dragon?" Hildr blurts.

Odin gives her a strange look. "Do you not know anything about the gods?" Without waiting for an answer, he shakes his head and continues, "Yes, Loki can. He's a shape-shifter, enabling him to transform into many different shapes and sizes." He stops pacing and focuses on me. "Back to the subject. The emperor dragon owes us a baby, at least, if not two. This is a good place to start. The dragon that you've been riding is ours. It's vicious, and you must turn it over to the Valkyries. Do you understand?"

"Yes, I understand." I nod once.

"And if anyone deserves to ride an emperor dragon…" He puffs out his chest. "It will be the gods. We are the only ones who deserve to ride the leader of the dragons."

Eir clears her throat, and hesitantly, with a small voice, she says, "Great Odin, that doesn't seem fair. This isn't a just repayment for the good that this dragon has done for us. The dragon does not wish to harm us. She wishes us peace. We should let her remain free."

Odin glares at Mistress Sigrun. "I didn't know that you are raising dragon sympathizers within this Valkyrie Academy. This must stop right this instant!"

The mistress's face pales. She shakes her head and holds up her hands. "This is not of my doing or the doing of any of the instructors. This purely comes down to Kara." She throws me a glare out of the corner of her eye and crosses her arms.

"I am not here to listen to blame games. If I don't have a dragon delivered to me within the week, other measures will be executed."

"What other measures?" I can't hide the worry in my voice.

"Pray that you do not find out, young Valkyrie. It won't be pleasant." The great god spins around and glowers his disapproval at Mistress Sigrun before he exits the room.

Mistress Sigrun straightens her shoulders in a way that reminds me of a duck shaking its body. "Well, Valkyries, you heard him. You must follow his instruction." She lifts her chin and follows Odin out the door.

- CHAPTER TWO -

Hildr slams the door behind Odin and
Mistress Sigrun. "That's ridiculous." She spins
around and places her hands on her hips.
"They can't take a dragon away. And besides,
it's you who's bonded with the dragon."

"You don't have to tell me." Crossing my
arms, I say, "I don't care if he's a god. I'm not
handing my dragon over. I'm going to tell
Elan."

"Can we come?" Eir asks. Her usually calm eyes look anxious and keen at the same time. "I've never known that they can be peaceful creatures, and this one sounds interesting."

"I'd love to come too." Hildr's freckly face is loaded with enthusiasm.

"Okay. I don't know how she'll react. It's not like she's an animal in a circus. No chains or cages are holding her away if she wants to attack."

I open the door to the hall to make sure that there is no sign of Odin or the mistress. When I'm sure that they are gone, I quietly make my way outside, with Hildr and Eir following closely behind. It feels ridiculous to be sneaking around the halls of the academy, but I have to go and see Elan and warn her of what Odin's intentions are.

The corridor branches off, and something catches my eye along the alternative pathway. Peering around the corner, I see Rota being aided by her winged Valkyrie friends, Prima and Mist, down the end of the hallway. Despite Valkyries' fast-healing bodies, she is still bandaged in many places. I'm not surprised after the beating she received from the frost giant. It probably broke most of the bones in her body from the way it was throwing her around.

After the reception from Odin and Mistress Sigrun, I don't know what her reaction will be, so I make sure we tiptoe quietly past her down the hallway. The last thing we need is for Rota and her friends to hear us while we exit the building.

We sneak around the back of the lounge chairs in the lobby, avoiding as much attention as we can. It is not prohibited for us to leave the building during the night, but I want as few eyes as possible seeing where we are going.

When we reach the main entrance, I release my pent-up breath and step into the darkness. Bright stars twinkle in the night sky, and a long line of light cascades from the full moon across the rugged land. The sharp peaks have an eerie glow under the moonlight, yet at the same time, it brings me a strange comforting feeling. This is my home, and it's what I've known all of my life. Under the moon's glow, the land almost looks like it's covered in snow. Tonight, it is only an illusion.

"Elan, where are you?" I say in a normal voice after we have passed hearing distance from the academy building. I figure she must've remained close as she was talking to me only minutes before Odin arrived.

A few moments pass before a golden glow catches my eye, and I turn to see her golden scales bathing under the full moonlight. I am awestruck by the beauty of her colors under the moon. She is a creature that has the potential to be so dangerous and a face that is hard and vicious to look at, yet she has chosen me.

She lifts her head and peers in our direction. Her face is set in a menacing expression, and her large horns protruding from the top and back of her head are daunting and even frightening for me to look at. I hear a gasp, and Hildr halts her footsteps while I continue toward Elan. Her golden-brown eyes focus on my two friends then back on me. For a moment, I almost think that it is her mother, not Elan, who lies in the moonlight. Unpleasantness plasters her face, and those golden-brown eyes hold a warning.

"Elan?" Even I sound hesitant as I call her name.

She nods once, and a puff of smoke exits her nostrils. She looks intimidating, and I had forgotten that I have only known her for such a short time. In her friendliness toward me, it didn't even occur to me that I may need to ask her for permission to show her to my friends.

"She… she looks like she's going to eat us." Hildr's voice sounds unusually meek behind me.

"Perhaps this was not such a good idea." Eir sounds equally intimidated.

As I look at the angry expression in Elan's eyes, the lack of thought slaps me across the face. I curse my ignorance. "My friends would like to meet you," I say hesitantly.

She snorts, and more smoke shoots out of her nostrils. Her large split irises hold no compassion. The silence is painful as she stares at me for a moment longer before she eventually nods once. *Very well.* A serious tone dominates her voice, and my steps falter. She looks so much like her mother when she does that.

I am no longer confident about my actions. "Are you sure that's okay?"

She exposes her teeth, vast and menacing, and I flinch. A strange sound exits her mouth, and her tone changes. *I'm just kidding. Sure. They can come over. I don't mind.* Humor dances in her eyes. *Did you like my mother's impression? Was I intimidating?*

With the sudden release of tension, I almost collapse to my knees. I can't imagine what Hildr and Eir have gone through. "Very." I steer confidence back into my steps as I approach her and raise my hand to stroke her nose.

She leans into my touch. *You know, it's very unusual for us to like being touched like this.*

"You are a very unusual dragon," I say and smile. My hand travels along her snout and up to her horns, and I pull at them playfully. "You rascal! You scared the soul out of my friends."

Did I? Elan giggles, and her head jerks with the movement. *I know I did. I can see it on their faces.*

Hildr and Eir keep their distance while watching us interact. They would only be able to hear my side of the conversation as Elan speaks in my mind.

She stops giggling, and with her teeth still showing, she focuses on my friends cowering in the distance. Her eyes narrow. Looking like this, she is more intimidating. A voice deep and menacing projects through my head which I'm sure she is making sure the others hear as well. *What are you staring at?*

At first, I think she is still only talking to me, but her eyes are still focused on my friends. She stands abruptly and stomps toward them. *If you keep staring at me, I'll eat you for supper.*

Hildr and Eir back away from Elan's approach. Eir's foot catches on a rock, and she grasps Hildr as she stumbles, pulling her to the ground with her.

Refusing to take her eyes off Elan, Hildr reaches for her sword, and metal sliding against metal rings through the air as she pulls it from its sheath. The dragon has taken it too far.

"Elan!" I call, trying to stop her.

She throws her head back and cackles, the strange sound filling our surroundings and rumbling through our heads. Hildr's and Eir's jaws drop, and shocked relief washes over their expressions.

A second later, Hildr's relieved expression turns to anger, and she glares at Elan. "That's not funny." She aggressively thrusts her sword back in its sheath.

Eir's hand covers her heart. "Oh Vanir! I almost peed my pants."

Elan looks at me. *I thought you said these guys are warriors.* Her face fills with disbelief.

I raise my eyebrows. "We are. But I said you are friendly, and they weren't expecting you to attack. You need to be realistic. Look at the size difference between us. You are enormous. Besides, we haven't been taught how to fight dragons. It is only something that the winged Valkyries are allowed to do. But don't get me wrong… now that I have met you, I am glad that we haven't been fighting dragons. Perhaps we can work together differently."

Hildr has regained her composure, and she stares at Elan. "Can I climb on your back?"

At first, Elan looks startled, then she bares her teeth, and a hiss escapes her mouth.

"Elan!" I chastise her.

She glances at me out of the corner of her eye, and I see the mischief there. Then she pulls her lips over her teeth and buckles her front legs. *Sure. Be my guest.*

Excitement dances in Hildr's eyes as she observes Elan's posture when she tilts down so that Hildr will have an easier time to climb on. "Really?"

Absolutely. I don't see why not. After all, it is my body and my choice. Elan tilts her shoulder down closer to Hildr's height.

Eyes sparkling, Hildr approaches Elan, grabs her scales, and yanks herself up. It takes a lot of effort because the dragon is so big. Using her warrior strength, Hildr reaches into her core and uses her stomach muscles to pull her legs and torso over the dragon. When the struggle is over, she sits up straight on Elan's back and runs her hands over the golden scales along the dragon's shoulders.

Are you holding on? Elan peers over her shoulder at Hildr.

Hildr reaches forward and circles her arms around Elan's neck, clasping her scales. Elan bends her knees and pushes off the ground, flapping her long membranous wings until she reaches a decent height then soars through the air. Hildr's screams of enthusiasm reverberate through the valley while Elan flies a short circuit. After circling a few times, she spreads her wings and glides down to stop, landing stably on all four feet directly on the spot she ascended from. Her wings spread wide, and the spikes on the edges of her wings narrowly miss us as she tucks them away in time.

"Oh Vanir! That was awesome!" Hildr remains on Elan's back, transfixed to the spot, staring at the scales, her face full of awe. "We can't let Odin take her. She's amazing."

What? Elan's eyes widen with surprise, and she looks at me. *What is she talking about?*

"That's why Odin came to visit me. He is furious that I won't hand you over to Mistress Sigrun. He has demanded that I give you to him within a week."

Elan bounces to her feet, and the process knocks Hildr off her shoulders. When Elan realizes what she's done, she holds out her wing just in time to catch Hildr and stop her falling to the ground. She tilts her wing, cupping Hildr within it, and places her gently on the ground. *You can't be serious, can you?*

"Unfortunately, it's true," Eir says with a placid voice.

"Don't worry. I'm not going to let him take you. I'm certainly not handing you over," I say, placing a hand on her snout again. After a few strokes, she seems to relax slightly.

Hildr moves beside me. Her face is still awash with excitement as she looks up at Elan. "I will never let that happen. In fact, I would love a dragon of my own. Do you think you have a spare one somewhere?"

Elan giggles and nudges Hildr with her snout. *You're funny. Like my mother's going to do that. She will never hand over another dragon to the Valkyries other than what the alliance requires.*

My mind races with ideas. "Wait. What about one of the new dragons that have been received this year? What about the blue dragon, Naga? He is one we already have access to."

Hildr clasps her hands together. It is the most excited I remember seeing her. "Brilliant idea!"

Elan looks thoughtful. *To be honest, I think he would love to have someone to be with. He's rather playful.*

"Fantastic! A lively one," Hildr says excitedly. "Perhaps he can bring down frost giants too."

Maybe, Elan says. *I'll talk to him.*

"Sounds great! Just keep away from Odin. Okay?" I give her a warning look. "We should get back before someone notices we are gone."

We turn to leave, and she heads toward the dragon stalls.

- CHAPTER THREE -

The next morning, I hear from Elan, and I run to Hildr's bed and shake her awake.

She rolls over and smacks me in the face.

"Ow! I'm doing you a favor." I chuckle with disbelief. "You're always such a grouch in the morning."

"Yeah, you know I'm not a morning person." She flings her body into a sitting position and plunks her feet on the ground.

"Why are you waking me up so early anyway?"

"Elan has spoken to me. She talked with Naga, the blue dragon, last night. He is keen to meet you. So we'd better get out there before anyone notices we're missing."

"Really?" Her face suddenly comes to life, pushing aside all signs of drowsiness. She runs to the basin and splashes water over her face then grabs her sword from her bedside and straps the sheath on her belt.

"You won't need that. This is a friendly dragon."

Her eyes set in determination. "You never know what might come up. You should know that from training."

"You're right." I throw my quiver of arrows and my bow over my back and latch my sling over my back pocket. It has come in handy in the past when I have least expected it.

Eir hears the commotion, and her eyes crack open a sliver. "What's going on?" She rubs her eyes and slowly sits up.

"Hildr is going to meet Naga, the blue dragon. Did you want to come?" I adjust my quiver into a better position.

"Sure." She splashes some water on her face and follows us.

We weave our way through the boulders and over the rugged landscape until we reach the dragon stalls. It is a fair walk but nothing for our fit bodies.

The sun starts to push up over the horizon, and Hildr breaks into a jog. "I don't want to miss this. I want to see what it's like to have a dragon."

In an attempt to keep up, Eir and I break into a jog behind her.

When we reach the dragon stalls, Hildr pauses. "Which one is it?"

"It's in the one you found me in the other day when I was cleaning the stalls."

"The one that you patted on the snout?" she asks, peering at me over her shoulder.

"Yes, that one. Under the instruction of Elan, he had been playing with me just before you arrived. But I don't think he needed the instruction from Elan. He seemed to enjoy it anyway. He's like a big dog."

We run down the corridor, and she leads us straight to the door where they had found me the other day. In a combined effort, we slide the door across and see the dragon facing the door and standing to attention in the middle of the room. When he sees me walk in, his eyes widen, and his tail starts to wag.

I walk in cautiously, waiting for the plume of fire to shoot my way. I hold up my hands. "Remember, no plumes of fire. Okay? They hurt us."

The dragon nods enthusiastically, his flat head a symbol of friendliness.

"He's tiny compared to Elan," Hildr says, walking in cautiously behind me.

"Yes, but I'm sure he can still carry your weight." I spot Eir following Hildr into the room, then I go up to Naga and put my hands around his neck and lean over his head. I carefully rub him on the snout and tickle his forehead. A strange bubbling comes from his neck, and I pull my face away from his head before he jerks it upward and shoots it down, snorting out a plume of fire.

"Vanir!" Hildr cries. She darts out of the way just in time. Her eyes flick to the dragon. "Is that what he calls friendly?"

"He must have forgotten that plumes of fire can hurt us." I look up into the blue dragon's eyes, and they are wide with shock. "It doesn't look as though he meant it."

Hildr eyes him suspiciously as though trying to read his face for understanding. She approaches him hesitantly before being cut off by Eir as she rushes forward.

Eir stares at the dragon with wide-eyed amusement and strokes him on the nose. "Oh,

the poor thing! He definitely didn't mean that."
Then she strokes him down the neck.

Hildr takes another step toward him and
rubs his nose. I hear another rumble in his
throat and pull away. Before I can shout a
warning, his head jerks up then down again,
and he spits out another plume of fire in
Hildr's direction. She jumps aside, and the
plume narrowly misses her.

The blue dragon's eyes are wide. He almost
looks regretful.

"What is wrong with him?" Hildr protests.
"It's the second time he's nearly got me with a
plume of fire. I thought he was supposed to
know that it's dangerous to us." Her face fills
with annoyance until she sees that his is full of
regret. "He looks uncertain. Why is he not
speaking to me? Does he not understand us?"

"I don't know," I say. "I guess after being
with Elan, I just expect them all to speak
English. If he can understand what you want

but doesn't speak the same language, does that matter?"

Suddenly, a puff of smoke shoots out of the dragon's nose, this time shooting just a few feet away from Hildr.

"Vanir!" she cries.

I search the dragon's eyes for the reason. "Wait. I think the poor guy has a cold." I pet him on the nose and around the holes for his ears. "Do you have a cold, my dear little dragon?"

His big blue eyes dart my way, and he nods. *Yes, I'm sorry. I is sick. My English not good. But I still play.* His eyes widen with enthusiasm.

Eir shuffles over to him and hugs his nose. "He's adorable, Hildr. You have to give him another chance."

Hildr stands poised in front of him for a few moments, her eyes fixed on him in contemplation. Then her shoulders slump. "All right. I'll give him another chance." She approaches him, and his tail begins to wag.

Yeah. Yeah. I can play! I can play! His voice passes through all our heads at the same time.

A smile almost breaks across Hildr's face before being interrupted by the dragon's head suddenly tilting up then down again. Another plume of fire shoots right at her. She jumps to the side. "Vanir! This one is going to keep me on my toes."

I sorry. The dragon gives her a wide-eyed look. *I didn't mean it.*

Hildr dusts her leather sleeve and looks at him. Her eyes are full of distrust and annoyance. But after a few moments, she pulls herself together and says, "That's okay. We shall try again." Her voice isn't joyful, but I can tell that she's willing to give him another go, especially seeing as she's determined to ride a dragon and have a formidable partner with her in battle. She looks up at him and spreads her arms wide. "Let's play."

The blue dragon stands and wags his tail, and I get out the way with Eir following my example. Naga's whole backside is swaying with the motion before he pushes off and sprints toward Hildr. At first, I think he is moving in for a cuddle—until I suddenly realize that he's not about to stop. He slams straight into Hildr, knocking her onto her back.

"Vanir!" She slowly climbs to her feet, rubbing her backside to get the feeling back into her rear end while glaring at the dragon. Then she holds up her arms. "I can't do this today. I've had enough. I'll try again later." She turns and promptly exits the stall.

- CHAPTER FOUR -

I pet Naga on the nose and scratch him behind his ears. "It's okay. I'll go talk to her."

Eir strokes him on the nose and follows me out of the stall, and we close the big solid rock door behind us. As we walk down to the stone hallway, we see no sign of Hildr. She has stomped off so quickly that she has completely disappeared and left us behind.

I turn to Eir. "I'm going to talk briefly to Elan. I'll meet you at the breakfast hall."

Eir nods and makes her way back to the Valkyrie Academy building, and I head off, looking for Elan, but I can't see her golden scales glimmering anywhere in the rising sun. I travel to where we met her last night, and I can't see her there either. I call loudly enough to be heard by her but not so loudly that the academy can hear me. "Elan?" I wish I could speak to her directly in her head. It would be much easier to hold a conversation without being noticed than having to say everything out loud. "Elan?" I call again when I don't hear an answer. I continue to search for her, hoping to spot some sign of her. While continuing to call her name, I travel a full circle of the academy but with no luck. After fifteen minutes of searching, I shrug and head back to the hall to have breakfast.

When I arrive at the hall, I search for Hildr and Eir and spot them at a table in the far corner. Their plates are loaded with food, and they have started eating. I grab a plate, pile food on it, and go sit with them.

"What did Elan say?" Eir asks.

"I can't find her."

"*What?*"

"I kept looking and calling to her, but she never responded and never showed."

"Is she all right?" Hildr's eyes cloud with concern. The short visit with Elan has apparently impacted her significantly and made her fall in love with the dragon.

"She should be. I don't see why she wouldn't be. She's probably just gone for a little trip off the grounds and will be back later. Or maybe she's even gone to tell her mother a few things. I don't know. She's a free dragon." Tingles run down my spine, giving me the feeling that someone is watching me. I glance around and see Mistress Sigrun staring at me with a conceited look on her face, almost victorious.

Hildr and Eir follow my gaze.

"She looks rather happy this morning." Hildr grunts.

"Is there such a thing?" I ask. "Especially when looking at us." Coldness creeps over my shoulders as I stare back at the mistress. I try to shrug it off. "It's probably just a warning look that she is coming to take my dragon if I don't hand her over. Well, she can wait, and she can die waiting. It is not going to happen." I take a mouthful of food and swallow it without chewing. "I'm so annoyed. I could really do with something to work out some of this aggression."

"Perfect timing." Hildr says. "We have combat training next, and we are fighting against the winged Valkyries."

"Perfect!" I say, then I scoff the rest of my food and rise to my feet. "I'm going to sit in the hall. This is one lesson I don't want to wait for." I march down the hall and to the combat room to find that the mistress is already there.

"You're early, Wingless."

I roll my eyes then squint at the mistress, dying to say something snarky back. Though I have been here for three years, she still doesn't call me by my name. "I didn't want to wait for combat, Mistress. I am keen to work off some aggression."

Her mouth straightens into a thin line. I think it is meant to be a smile that she has forgotten to turn up at the edges of her mouth, but with her, I'm not quite sure. "Well, this is the perfect place," she says. "Why wait until class starts? You can start with one of the winged Valkyries."

I glance over and see Prima, one of Rota's friends. And even though I saved Rota the other day, her face is still covered in a sneer. The disdain for the wingless Valkyries is evident on her face, no matter how I tried to prove our worth that day.

She grabs a baton off the shelf and swings it threateningly against her bare hand. "Come on, Wingless. Let me help you with that aggression. Or wait… maybe you can help me with *my* aggression."

Without even waiting for me to collect a baton, she starts swinging hers and whacks me. I don't try to lunge for a weapon—I won't get there in time. A second later, she is already swinging the baton at me from the other direction. I dodge the hit, sliding down to the floor, and swing out my leg, which flicks around in a circle and knocks her feet from underneath her. She crashes to the floor onto her backside, and her weapon falls in her lap then clatters to the ground. She cries out from the impact but dusts herself off quickly and rises to her feet at the same speed as me.

I try to edge my way to the back of the room while keeping an eye on Prima. Even with her face screwed up into that horrible sneer, she still looks like a beauty queen. That beauty is skin deep, I'm sure. Underneath, she is as ugly as anything.

She holds the menacing stare and looks annoyed that she has already landed on the ground so early in the fight. When she swings the baton at me again, I dodge it. At the same time, I throw a fist at her face, and it connects with her chin. A loud crack sounds, and I can feel her jaw disconnecting from the force. She grimaces in pain as she labors to pull herself together and swings her baton at me. It connects with my forearm, and I hear a small snap. Pain shoots up to my head and down my fingers. I am sure that she has managed to fracture my arm. Thankfully, we have quick self-healing powers, one of the gifts that we have as a Valkyrie along with being immortal, but still, healing takes time. I have to pull myself together and prepare for another attack and get ready to retaliate. Putting the injured arm behind me, I skip in and deliver a roundhouse kick to the head.

I spin backward at the same time she swings the baton, and it collides with the shoulder of the same arm that is injured. I hear the snap as my collarbone breaks, and my arm goes limp. The pain is more intense than before, and I see stars. Before I know it, she raises the baton again, and she cracks it down on my head, which jerks and throbs with a splitting headache. I'm fortunate that I'm not falling to the ground, passed out. Though it is almost impossible for me to hold myself together and not to focus on the pain, I spin around and do a roundhouse kick to her head. I manage to knock her out, and she falls to the ground, her baton clunking to the floor.

Blood pours down my face and over my eye, and I wipe it away, leaving a smear on my forearm. It takes all my effort to remain on my feet, and I stumble. I place my legs shoulder width apart with my knees bent to hold me steady. Prima is still slumped on the ground, unmoving. My knees buckle, and my head lands cushioned in her white wings, before I pass out and dream of lying in white clouds.

- CHAPTER FIVE -

I am brought back to consciousness with a bucket of cold water.

"Wake up, sleepyhead." Hildr stands over me, the bucket still in her hand.

My head hits the floor with a thump, and I grimace then turn to realize that I was still lying on Prima's wing, and my cushioning disappeared when Rota pulled her up. I roll up into a sitting position. "Who won?"

Hildr huffs. "You were both knocked unconscious. I'm pretty sure that means you're about even."

I almost let out a cheer. My fighting skills have come a long way since I started at Valkyrie Academy. "That's a nice change." Stars circle my head, and I rub my forehead. "I always used to get my butt handed to me by those three."

"I don't know—I wouldn't really call that a victory." Hildr drains the last of the water in the bucket onto the floor.

"Yeah, but I knocked her out too. It wasn't just me being the unconscious one. To me, that's an improvement since the last time I fought against her, about a year ago." The stars diminish, and I look around the room some more. "How long have I been out?"

"Long enough for the class to start and for them to walk in and find you two passed out on the floor." Hildr huffs a laugh.

"Where is Mistress Sigrun?" I search the room, looking for the hard-faced mistress.

Hildr's eyes hold disbelief. "She left the room, leaving you two on the floor."

"I saw her leave just before we came in." Eir holds me by the shoulders to help stabilize me. "It's rather disconcerting that she would leave you both here and not put you somewhere better or try to help you recover quickly. We should take you to the wall."

I rub the spot on my head a bit more and wipe away some of the blood. "Yeah, well, I'm not surprised."

"It is shocking, as far as I'm concerned," Eir says as she and Hildr help me to the side of the room.

They lower me to the floor to sit against the wall while ignoring all the stares and sneers from the winged Valkyries. Despite it being an even match, they still see it as though I am less than them and will never have the fighting capability that they have. Considering we don't get as much combat training as they do, I am ecstatic.

"Take another beating, did we?" I look up to see Rota mocking me as I walk past.

Mist giggles. "Ha-ha. Yeah, the floor jumped up and beat her."

Rota glowers at Mist and her stupidity.

Hildr slides between us and puffs out her chest. "I would call it an even match, actually. Prima even had the advantage of wings, and she still can't beat her."

Placing a hand on Hildr's arm, I say, "Just leave it, Hildr. It's not worth it."

"I just so want to teach these winged imbeciles that we are greater than what they give us credit for. The fight was even. It's the only way to describe it. It's about time they learn this," she says through gritted teeth.

I rub my head where the wound is bleeding. Weariness is catching up to me. "I know."

Hildr hooks her arm under my shoulder. "Come on. Let's get you to the nurse."

Eir hunkers down and takes my other side. Together, they assist me down the corridor and into the nurse's quarters.

~~~~~

OUR HEALER STANDS with her back toward us and her head bent over a bench as she studies the things lying on top. It is a beautiful sight to see and a comfort that she has no wings. Her auburn hair falls in tight curls to her shoulders. Hearing our approach, she spins around to look at us. Her face is slightly weathered, the faint wrinkles around her eyes the only signs of her being older than the students. Yet she is still a picture of beauty.

"Hi, Anita," Hildr greets her as though everything is fine.

As her green eyes focus on us, her face softens. "I see you've been trying to teach the winged Valkyries a lesson again." Her voice is authoritative, yet a tone of understanding seeps through.

"It's about time they learned the lesson." Hildr escorts me to the nearest gurney then crosses her arms.

"This war between the winged Valkyries and the wingless has been going on for years, even before I was at the academy. Which, I must admit, is an extremely long time ago. I can't even remember the number of years." Anita chuckles. "The curse of an immortal life!" She shakes her head. "Never have the winged Valkyries given us more than menial duties."

Gawking at her, I say, "But you're a healer. You don't clean. You don't chase after them."

"I am a healer, yes, and I love doing what I do. It was an enormous effort that took a great deal of time and patience for me to get this far, and I only managed that because I had a natural talent. Eventually, after a lot of persisting, they allowed me to pursue my interest. I'm not sure that I am the highest-ranking wingless Valkyrie in the way that jobs go." She grabs a vial off the bench and starts to stir the contents with a glass spoon. "Don't get me wrong—I love what I do, but there was a time when I wanted to join the winged Valkyries and help reap souls for Valhalla. Never has the wingless Valkyrie managed to achieve that." After placing the vial down, the healer grabs a cloth and wipes the blood off my face and cleans my wound. She then grabs the vial and smooths the newly mixed paste over the sore before placing a butterfly closures over the split.

"Even so…" I gasp as she presses hard on either side of my sore to get the bandage to stick and seal it back together. "You have achieved great things by getting this far. It still gives us the inspiration to try to change their ways."

She lowers her face to my level, and sadness mixed with softness and understanding manifests in her eyes. "I have seen many come through who would like to prove them wrong and prove that we are worth more. But none have managed to succeed to that level." Anita turns around and places her equipment on the bench, and the glass spoon clatters against the vial. Then she turns back to me. "I wish you luck in doing that. I honestly do. It will be a breath of fresh air for that change. I am much older and enjoy my medicine too much to go into the fighting scene again although I will certainly support a cause. And, besides, I hear you did a great job yesterday fighting off a frost giant not only by yourself but also with a dragon." A question lies in her eyes.

"Yes, I did."

"I hope you know what you're doing. Dragons are very wild, unpredictable creatures. I would hate for you to become their dinner."

My mouth pushes up on one side. "Yes, I keep getting that message. At the moment, I think I will be more likely to become the

mother's dinner than the dragon that I ride.
She really is something else. I will take you to
meet her if I find her today."

"What do you mean, 'find her'?" Her brow
furrows with confusion.

"She seems to have disappeared. But I'm not
so worried at the moment. She's probably just
gone to visit her mother or take a break. It is
not like she's welcome here. On top of that,
Odin wants to capture her and enslave her."

Hildr's eyes widen with enthusiasm. "Yes,
she really is something else. I wish I had a pet
dragon. One that will let me ride it and fight
with it."

"We tried that this morning, remember? But
you got too impatient and stormed out." I
shake my head at Hildr.

"He kept shooting fireballs at me!" Hildr
flung her hands up in exasperation. "He wasn't
the brightest of creatures."

Eir looks at her with disappointment and pouts. "He was cute. You should have given him more chances. He had a head cold."

The healer observes Hildr and says, "I imagine you would have to get used to a little aggression if you want to deal with a dragon. Does Odin know that you are doing this, or Mistress Sigrun?"

I shake my head. "No, and please don't tell them. I don't want them to know. It could ruin everything for our plans. And besides, there is no guarantee that Hildr will bond with the dragon."

"I'll help where I can," Anita says.

"Thank you." A thought shoots into my head, and I gasp. "Hildr, I think there is another dragon we could try."

Hildr's body straightens, and her wide eyes focus on me, her face a mask of shock. "One of the dragons? Aren't they all vicious in there?"

"There was one that didn't attack me, and it still looked quite young. There is a chance that we could try that one."

- CHAPTER SIX -

"*H*ildr, wait up!" Eir calls, holding her chest and puffing.

Though we are just as fit as Hildr, we are both puffing, trying to keep up with her. She has left us behind in her excitement to meet this new dragon.

I'd forgotten that they hadn't had to clean out the dragon stalls, as they were mostly given other menial tasks like housekeeping or scrubbing the floors. It is rumored that cleaning the dragon pens is the most disgusting job and the most dangerous, making the majority of the Valkyries afraid to go near the stalls. Because of my fascination with them, I push aside these concerns so that I can interact with them.

I call to Hildr, "Do you even know which stall you're going to?"

Hildr slows down slightly. "Sure, one of the ones with a dragon in them."

"True, but there are hundreds of them." I don't hide my disbelief.

Her excitement doesn't waver. "Then one of the ones in the newer area."

"There is a new area?" I ask in a mocking tone.

Hildr slows her pace and keeps in step with us. We all pant while we continue forward down the stone corridor until we reach the door to the dragon stall that I believe holds the dragon. I help Hildr roll the door open, and she sticks her head inside. A massive roar bellows through the door, and she pulls her head back just before a plume of fire shoots her way.

With wide eyes, Hildr faces me. "Is this the one? Because it doesn't seem too friendly. Even the old dummy down the hall has friendlier plumes of fire than this one."

Cautiously, I quickly stick my head around the corner to make sure it is the right dragon. Inside is a massive yellow dragon with horns pointing upright. It lacks the golden tinge of the emperor dragon and is thinner in size, but this one still appears quite intimidating. When it sees me, it points its horns in my direction, ready to charge. It peers defiantly at me with a look threatening death.

I pull my head back and duck behind the door, slapping my hand over my panting chest. "Well." I pant some more. "That's not the stall."

Hildr rolls her eyes, and they help me move the door across the entrance.

Looking down the corridor, I calculate the doors in my head, trying to remember which one is the correct one. I point to each one, counting silently in my head. "Actually, I think it's that one." I chuckle slightly. It is the stall next to the one we just opened.

We approach the door and pull it open. This time, Hildr sticks her head in more cautiously.

When she doesn't pull it back within seconds, I stick my head around the corner as well and peer in. Leaning against the far wall, with his big brown eyes looking sad and sorrowful, is the same brown dragon with the big gash down his leg and no muzzle over his nose.

"Yes, this is the one."

His scales are the color of mud. Two large horns protrude from the crown of his head with a mane of smaller horns covering the back of his head and the top of his neck.

Eir sticks her head around the corner. "Oh, the poor thing! Look at his leg. That's a horrible sore."

The gash looks worse than it did yesterday. A red circle surrounds it, and it appears bigger and puffier. It is showing all the signs that it is infected.

"I can't believe how they mistreat these dragons. They're living creatures. They deserve to be looked after." Hildr pushes into the stall.

The dragon's eyes are wide with caution and distrust as he watches us. I don't blame him after the way the winged Valkyries have treated him. He remains pressed against the stone wall, watching me. It is the same thing that he did when I entered to clean the stall yesterday.

As we move closer, he spreads his wings, which are attached to his front arms like bat wings. I have not seen this on the other dragons.

"Don't worry," I say in a soothing voice. "We're not here to hurt you. We're just here to see if we can make friends." I take a couple more steps toward him while holding my hand up, palm facing the dragon. "I don't know if you can understand me, but I have just made friends with an emperor dragon."

Though I'm not sure if it's me or my imagination, I think I see a flicker of disbelief in his eyes.

I edge farther forward. "No, no, it's true. I really have, and she's allowed me to ride her. Together, we are working on building the trust between the Valkyries and the dragons. We are starting with my friends. They want to make peace with the dragons and get to know them."

The dragon still looks at me with disbelief in his eyes. He must understand me, and he has a level of intelligence that Naga, the blue dragon, doesn't seem to have.

Hildr pushes forward, bypassing me, and the brown dragon pulls back and watches her with curious eyes. When she steps within a few feet of the dragon, a low rumble rolls up his throat.

"Careful," I warn her. "That was a warning rumble that it is about to shoot fire."

Hildr braces, ready to move, but her excitement is pulling her toward this dragon, even after the warning that she is approaching too quickly. She must be able to see the intelligence in his eyes compared to Naga's. She slowly moves a step closer. "Hey, big guy. I am just trying to make friends. I'm not trying to hurt you at all. In fact, I want to help."

The dragon shifts his head to the side, spits out a small plume of fire, then looks back at Hildr. It is almost like he is telling her that he doesn't believe her. The intelligence outweighs the age.

"It's true, big guy. This is one of my friends. She is not like the winged Valkyries." I move in line with Hildr. "This pact that has been made between the dragons and the Valkyries is not fair, especially to you and the other sacrificial dragons handed over. Perhaps if we work together, we can break this alliance and live in peace together."

Hildr extends her arm slowly toward the dragon at the same time as taking a cautious step forward. The dragon's chains around his ankles clank against the stone floor as he pulls away.

When Hildr goes to take another step, a voice rings in my head.

Stop. The voice is loud and clear.

"Did you hear that, Hildr?" I ask, warning her before she takes another step forward.

"Yes," she says, looking disappointed.

"I heard it too." Eir moves to stand next to me.

The dragon continues to watch Hildr. It hasn't sent out a plume of fire yet, so I take that as a good sign.

Hildr moves her feet a few inches forward, and the dragon tilts his head up in annoyance.

Hildr balks. "I promise I'm here to be your friend."

The dragon raises his head higher as though to emphasize his dominance.

Then stop. The voice rings through our heads again. *You must come no farther. I do not trust your kind, and if you wish to gain my trust as a friend, you must do as I say to prove yourself.*

Hildr pauses, doing what the dragon commanded. She doesn't look as though she is about to make another move forward and is listening to the dragon. This is good.

A horn blares in the distance, and instantly, my ears prick up. "I'm off, guys. I'll catch you later."

"What?" Hildr looks dumbfounded.

"You've got this. You don't need me. I bonded with my dragon on my own through communicating. This is good."

"Yes, but where are you off to?" Hildr asks, not taking her eyes of the dragon. A wise move.

"I'm off to find Elan," I say.

"You'd better not be chasing after that horn," Hildr says.

"You know me too well." I smirk at her over my shoulder.

"They're not going to let you through," Hildr calls back.

"I know. But perhaps I can get through with Elan."

"And how do you expect to pull that off?" Hildr asks.

"Perhaps I can fly through at the same time as the winged Valkyries."

Eir shakes her head.

"Don't get into mischief," I call.

"I wasn't about to run off and get myself into trouble like you are," Hildr calls back.

"They have to catch me first," I say as I run out of the enclosure.

- CHAPTER SEVEN -

While hurrying away from the dragon stalls, I search everywhere for Elan. I can't see her anywhere. I call, "Elan? Where are you?" It would be so much easier if I could speak in her mind as she does in mine. I run around until I reach the spot I saw her last night. "Elan! Where are you?" I call again between the blare of the horns.

A flock of Valkyries flies over me and heads straight for Heimdall's point for the entrance of

Bifrost. I wish I could find my dragon and join them. Searching high and low, I run around the academy another time. I am constantly distracted by the Valkyries flocking to the entrance of Bifrost. I spot Rota and her friends flying together toward the departure spot. Again, it pulls at my heartstrings. Even though I helped save Rota and stopped her from being harmed any further by the frost giant, they still do not see me as equal and still want to belittle me. Searing pain shoots through my shoulder and my arm, and I peek at my scarred shoulder and rub it.

Another shadow passes over me, and I glance up, expecting to see another winged Valkyrie. Instead, I spot the creature that attacked Heimdall—the one that scratched my arm. I'm about to drop to the ground and hide behind a boulder when I realize it isn't interested in me. It is flying in an odd direction away from the bottom of Odin's castle, away from the depths of the mountain. I can't help but think that this is odd. It is a mystery to me how it is flying around so freely when I have been telling people about it. Surely, they must've gone to look for it now, and I'm not the only one who has seen it. Heimdall has also seen it and told Odin about it. I rub my shoulder and keep searching for Elan.

Another horn blares, and I give up my fruitless search for Elan. It's incredible how much I miss her, even though I've only known her for such a short time. She is so amazing, and the fact that she's chosen me makes my longing for her more like an addiction.

I have little time left to catch the opening to Midgard before the blare of the horn stops, so I start the climb up the sheer face of the mountain. I claw, push, and drag myself up until, finally, I reach the edge of the cliff, where I hook my fingers into a crevice and throw a leg over the side, yanking myself up. My back arches as I crouch on all fours. Slowly, I stand

and regain my breath, only to be met with Heimdall's glare of disappointment.

"Young wingless Valkyrie! What are you doing back here?" His feet are shoulder width apart, and his fists are on his hips. His horned helmet casts an eerie shadow over me. "You know you cannot be here."

My shoulder aches some more, and I instantly start looking for the creature, but it never shows. I rub my shoulder then look back at Heimdall. "Please, I just want help to prove myself. I helped with the frost giant that entered Asgard. I thought that they would also let me help in Midgard."

Sympathy and compassion flash across his face, unlike the first reception I got when I tried to get through the gate. It is only for an instant, then that expression flees. The huge gatekeeper pulls his shoulders back and stands to attention. "No. I cannot allow you to pass."

My shoulders slump. "Are you serious? I have worked so hard for this."

"I'm sorry, young Valkyrie. I cannot let you pass. It is forbidden."

Something flickers, and I turn to see a black silhouette forming in the middle of Bifrost's lights. At first, I frown, then my eyebrows rise. It's only seconds before I can feel my cheeks burning. Standing within Bifrost's light is a young male wearing all-black clothes, and two beautiful black wings protrude from his back.

"Harut," I whisper in confusion. I forgot how good-looking he is.

His eyes land on me, and his mouth presses into a smile. He looks as though he is in Asgard, yet at the same time, he doesn't seem to be here. Almost as though he is a hologram.

"What are you doing here?"

He remains in that spot, still smiling. I move toward the entrance of the building, and Heimdall blocks my way with one big step.

"My friend Harut, an angel of death, is here." I point at Harut. "I want to go see him."

Heimdall crosses his arms. "You are not going to distract me that easily."

I pout. "But I'm telling you the truth."

"Whatever you say. I'm not falling for it." Heimdall shakes a finger at me.

I shake my head then try to go around him. Again and again, he maneuvers and blocks my way.

"Return to the academy, young Valkyrie. This is not a place for you."

When I peer at the portal of Bifrost, Harut is gone. I stop trying to push my way past. I couldn't be more downhearted than I am right now. I am denied entrance into Midgard, I'm not allowed to talk to my unusual friend, and I can't find my beautiful dragon. Feeling dejected, I turn around. My journey back to the academy is a lot slower than my way there.

I stop at the academy, looking for my friends. They aren't in the room, so I try the mess hall and classes. When I come up empty-handed, I try the dragon stalls and head back to the one I left them in. It's open, and I stick my head around the corner before I enter. Hildr is still trying to get through to the dragon. She doesn't seem to have made any progress since I was there. She is still standing the same distance away.

"How's it going?"

"You're back early. How did it go?" Eir asks.

"The usual story."

The dragon's back is straight, as though he's standing at full attention. Every so often, he casts a warning look at Hildr. He isn't moving any closer, nor is he backing away.

"He won't let me in any farther, and he won't move," Hildr says, sounding annoyed and disappointed. As though to emphasize the point, she moves her feet a few inches forward, and a deep growl rumbles out of the dragon's throat.

"What's his name?" I ask.

"How am I supposed to know?" Hildr snaps.

Eir smiles softly. "She's been too busy trying to get closer and hasn't asked him too many questions."

"You could start with a conversation to build up trust. Perhaps after the dragon gets to know you, he might relax a bit."

I notice a mess that is new since I cleaned his stall yesterday. "Another way to help him out would be to clean up his stall." The dragon's sore is weeping and looks to be getting worse. "And perhaps you could show that you care by going to get something to help ease the pain of the sore and help it heal faster," I suggest.

Hildr slaps her palm on her forehead and groans. "Argh! I've been so stupid. Of course, all these things would help. I've been so busy trying to get close to him and pet him that it completely wiped all these other ideas from my mind."

I shrug. "In the meantime, I'm going to try to find Elan and ask her if she has tips or can come and talk to him. I'll talk to you later." I walk out, leaving her and Eir to clean up the stall.

A fair amount of time has passed since I last looked for Elan. Perhaps she has come back. I cling to hope and spend more time walking around, calling to her, but I still don't find her. It is just my luck to have a dragon that can disappear and turn invisible. I wish she were always visible to me.

Passing through a group of jagged mountains, I hear something up ahead. I follow it around the curve of the mountain and turn left when something catches my eye. A clatter sounds as I approach the place, confirming that I didn't imagine the first sound. After all the calling to Elan I did before this, I have hopes that she is here. Maybe she has finally heard me.

I weave my way around the cliff faces of the jagged mountain and turn another corner only to stumble across an old lady. She looks haggard and worn as though the years haven't been kind to her. It is an unusual sight after living at the academy for so long. All the Valkyries look so young, even the old ones. The gods have blessed us with beauty and long life.

Studying her, I move a little closer. "Who are you? I haven't seen you around."

The woman comes close to me and raises a gnarly finger lined with too many wrinkles to count. They even cover her knobbly knuckles, which bulge so much that they look deformed. "There are many people on Asgard, my dear." Her eyes are dark, and they have a strange intelligence behind them. "And many that you will not know. I am just one."

Though I don't argue because I know it is true, I struggle with her age. It is such an unusual thing. I would think that I would remember someone so different from the majority of people of Asgard. I can't pull my eyes away from her. "Are you lost out here?"

"I could ask you the same thing." The old woman smiles, showing her gappy brown teeth, then reaches out and touches my shoulder, and I pull away. She gives me a strange look then shrugs and points at my shoulder. "What is that?"

I look at where she is pointing and notice that some of the scar that the creature gave me is showing. A strange sensation runs through the scar. I shrug. "It's just an old scar."

She studies it for a few moments. "It looks to be tainted with magic."

Frowning, I say, "I have no idea what you are talking about."

Her faded brown eyes continue to study me, and she arches an eyebrow with a look of amusement. "This may bring you many interesting things."

It occurs to me that she must be some kind of witch. Perhaps she has dark-elf blood running through her veins, but I have not heard of any living in this part of Asgard.

Breaking the silence, she says, "I heard you call for something. What was it?"

Trying to assess whether I should tell her, I stare at her for a moment. I'm not sure how much I should tell her about the dragon.

She must spot my hesitation because she places a hand on my forearm. "Don't worry, dear. You can tell me. I am a friend of your mother."

I can't help frowning. I didn't think my memory of my mother was that bad. It has only been a few years since I permanently left home and moved to Valkyrie Academy. After careful consideration, I give in. I am sure that the rumors would have already started to spread. "I am looking for my dragon."

"A dragon, you say." She removes her hand from my forearm and clasps her other arm in front of her. "What an interesting thing. And what does this dragon look like?"

I think I see a gleam in the old woman's eyes, but I push it aside. "It is one with golden scales. The emperor kind."

She raises an eyebrow, exposing her faded dark eyes more.

I interpret this as her not believing me, and I blurt, "The dragon is only young." I wave a dismissive hand at her. "It's all right. You probably haven't seen it around here." The temptation to leave is great.

The woman raises a finger. "Ah, yes. Yes. I have. I have seen one of these dragons."

The hurry to leave has diminished for the moment. "Where? Was it recently?" My shoulders sag. "Or was it back when you were young?"

The woman chuckles. "It was recently." She leans in as though she is about to tell me a secret. "In fact, it was only today."

"Really?"

She nods. "I saw one at the bottom of Odin's castle. It is surrounded by guards and is deep down in the depths of the castle's grounds."

I gasp. "Really?"

Nodding with more enthusiasm, she asks, "This wouldn't happen to be your dragon, would it?"

"It better not be." But deep down, I have a suspicion that it may be Elan. I haven't seen her all day, and no other emperor dragons are in the area—unless Odin was lying. He made it clear that he didn't have his own emperor dragon. He must have found her and stolen her, even though they gave me a week to hand her over. "I have to get her back."

"Ah!" She nods once, her eyes full of understanding. "Good luck with that."

I spin around to leave then change my mind because I have another question I want to ask her. "How—" When I turn around, she has disappeared. Briefly, I search for her without success.

Around the next corner of the mountain, something catches my eye, and I glance over just in time to see the beast that tried to steal the dragon's egg take off into the sky. I dash to the side of the mountain and push my back up against it, trying to hide within its shape. Holding my breath, I watch as the creature flies away.

- CHAPTER EIGHT -

The hairs on the back of my neck rise as I watch the creature fly away. Only when I'm sure it's gone do I allow myself to move, contemplating the old woman and how this is a strange place to find her. I hope she makes it to her destination without the creature finding her.

With the creature gone, I leave my hiding spot and head back to the dragon stall. I search for my friends in the academy but come up empty-handed until, eventually, I find them in the dragon stall where I left them. Some progress has been made since I left, for when I enter, Hildr is past the barrier that the dragon had set for her, and she is now rubbing some cream over his leg. This is progress. As she rubs on some of the ointment, the dragon throws his head back then brings it forward. The salve must have a kick to it when applied. Hildr's face beams as she works.

"Is it starting to help?" Eir moves slightly closer.

"Of course. Did you expect it to do anything else?" Hildr places the lid back on the salve and looks at the dragon. "Does that mean I can pet you now?"

Don't push it. The dragon's brown eyes fill with warning.

"You can't blame me for trying." Hildr pulls her head back and grins at the dragon.

"You seem to be making some progress." I step farther into the stall, and Hildr and Eir jump then turn around to look at me.

Eir throws a hand over a heart. "You scared me. Where did you come from?"

"Sorry."

"Back so soon? Didn't you find her?" Hildr looks shocked.

"No. But in my search, something else came up, and I need your help."

"What is it?" Eir asks.

I glance at Hildr sitting close to her dragon and notice that he has dropped his guard some more. "Actually, it doesn't matter."

I turn to run off, but Hildr calls after me. "Where are you going?"

"I have to go and check something out."

"What?" Eir looks at me, concerned.

"Well, on the way back, I ran into an old woman."

"An old woman?" Hildr asks.

"Yes, an old woman. It was a strange meeting. She came out of nowhere, and she was extremely old. I don't remember seeing someone so old. In any case, she told me a dragon is tied up underneath Odin's castle. She didn't know if she saw my dragon, but she said it was a young emperor dragon that was tied up underneath the castle. I'm going to take a look."

"Are you mad?" Hildr almost yells at me.

Worry fills Eir's eyes. "It is definitely pushing the boundaries, going to Odin's castle uninvited to check out one of his prisoners."

"Yeah, but if it's her, he took her without my permission. Whether he likes it or not, she's *my* dragon, not his, and she is a free dragon."

"I'm coming with you." Hildr backs away from her dragon, and he gives her a funny look.

I shake my head. "No, you can stay with your dragon. Besides, it is going to be too dangerous, and I could even get myself expelled or worse. I'll meet you back here."

"Are you sure?" Hildr asks.

I nod at the dragon. "Spend some more time with him to see if you can bond some more. Hopefully, I'll find Elan."

~~~~~

MY HEART THUMPS rapidly as I head toward Odin's castle. With the mistress distracted by a mission, I don't have to worry about her interfering when she discovers that I am gone. The walk to the castle seems to take a long time. I am eager to see Elan again. On one hand, I hope it is her, but on the other hand, I hope it isn't. Either way, I have to find out.

It takes some effort to skip past the guards and avoid their attention as I sneak down the halls. My arm has been giving me funny sensations ever since the old woman touched me. I shake it, trying to get rid of this odd feeling, but it doesn't go away.

With my back pressed firmly against the wall, I manage to sneak past the guards at the entrance of the castle, and head for the lower levels. I have never been down here before, though that is a good thing—it means that I haven't been locked up in the palace. I have heard they're quite nasty to the imprisoned.

It takes quite some time to pass the kitchen and the laundry and wind farther down into the dark, windowless depths of the palace. If Elan is down here, it must be so drab and dreary for her after coming from the wild.

I make my way down the corridors, dodging past more guards and holding my breath until I am confident they are gone. After a while, I notice that I haven't seen a guard for some time. I take a deep breath in and decide to risk it. I say in a normal voice but not too loudly, "Elan." Pressing my back against the wall, I rest my head against the solid form, wanting to capture some of its security. I try to still my thumping heart. I don't hear any scuffling of guards coming my way, so I take a deep breath and try again, and this time, my voice is slightly louder. "Elan."

There is no answer. I let out a long breath. I had hoped that the dragon would hear me and respond. Though I still don't know if she's the one that I am trying to rescue and risking my freedom for.

Moving along the halls, I reach a lower level with all kinds of creatures in it. As I stealthily move past the creatures, I keep an eye out for one that looks like the creature that marked me. Perhaps it isn't the only one. But nothing like it is locked up here.

I push through until I see several guards run into one of the stalls with spears aiming forward. A steady rumble shakes the solid foundation of the floor, followed by an enormous roar. A large plume of fire shoots through the bars at the guardsmen standing menacingly outside. From the intense flames that burst through, I know it has to be a dragon.

Peering through the bars, I spot a large and intimidating golden dragon. Its screams of rage promise demise to all who approach it. A couple of bloodstains on its chest weep from holes large enough to be caused by spearheads. They don't appear to be deep, just enough to let the dragon's blood flow. Its face is so full of anger and threats that it reminds me of Elan's mother. Perhaps they have a different dragon. After all, Elan had other siblings. I'd never asked if they had hatched.

The dragon's slitted golden-brown eyes narrow, then it shoots out another massive plume of fire, narrowly missing the guards. A guard wipes the sweat away from his forehead as he backs a couple steps away. At first, I can't understand why the guards are trying to combat this captured dragon, but I spot another guard lying unconscious in the back corner of the room. I retreat around a corner and wait, listening to the guards' struggle.

After quite some time, a guard calls, "Retreat. We'll have to try again later. Maybe when she is asleep. There is no way she is going to let us through to get him."

After they pass, I peek around the corner and into the cage. The dragon stomps over to a pile of meat lying on the floor and devours several pieces. Her scales on her forehead are bunched together into a frown, and her eyes hold a look of aggression.

My body shakes as I move on silent feet to stand in front of the bars. The uncertainty is rocking me to my core. I hold my breath and brace myself, ready to dash to the side. The dragon is uncannily like Elan, and with this expression, she looks very much like Elan's mother.

After watching for a moment, I decide to take the risk. "Elan?"

The dragon stops eating, and the golden-brown eyes focus on me, her jaw still hovering over another piece of meat. The intense stare she is giving me makes me want to back away. Eventually, she blinks. *Kara?*

My breath releases with a loud gush. I would know that voice anywhere. "Yes. I'm so glad I found you."

Me too. How did you like the impersonation of my mother? Did you like it? Did you like it? I think I had the guards convinced. They were certainly running for their lives. She approaches the cage, and I reach out my hand, and she nuzzles it.

"You nearly had me running for my life. I started to think a different dragon was down here."

She laughs heartily, the noise rumbling up her throat. *So it worked then! I even had* you *fooled.*

"Yes, you even had *me* fooled. Now, though, we need to get you out of here." I pull my hand back and angle my body so I can slide through the bars. My black leather clothes squeak against them.

I approach the unconscious guard and search his pockets. "What happened to him?"

She looks at the ground. *Um. He kind of ran into my tail. Is he all right?*

"Ran into your tail, huh?" I say with sarcasm then feel for a pulse. "He'll be fine. Probably just a concussion."

Oh. Phew! I didn't mean to hurt him. Honest.

I continue searching his pockets until I finally hear the rattle of metal and pull out a loop of keys and set to work on the lock. It takes several keys before the lock finally pops and the door opens slightly.

"Got it." I leave the keys hanging from the lock and open the door wider.

Oh, you're awesome! Elan stoops her head down and nudges my chest. It is only then that I notice the big metal collar around her neck.

"I've been so worried about you. You just disappeared. I didn't know where you were. I thought that you might have gone to your mother's and decided not to come back."

Yeah, I forgot to make myself invisible after you left. I was snoozing, and they pounced on me with a tranquilizer and a net. It was a massive net, too, and I got all tangled up in it when they dragged me here.

"That makes sense." I hug her head, avoiding her horns, then retrieve the keys from the door and unlock her collar. "I was wondering how they managed to find you." Pocketing the keys, I set the collar on the ground.

We make our way out of the cell and down the corridor.

"Don't forget to turn invisible this time. We need to get you out of here."

- CHAPTER NINE -

*T*he passageway of the palace is enormous, except its size is nothing in comparison to the size of Elan. Although she is treading softly, the floor still shudders with every step. It is going to be extremely difficult to bypass all the soldiers with her massive bulk rocking the palace. Up ahead, some guards block the way, and I halt. A crunch sounds behind me.

"What are you doing?" I whisper.

She responds with a groan. Instinct tells me to turn around and have a look, but this would be pointless. Elan is still invisible, and it would be impossible to see what she is doing.

Sorry. I'm still drowsy from the dart that they hit me with. It was some potent stuff. It's taking a while to wear off.

"Do you mean the tranquilizer they shot you with?" I listen to the noise of the guards, hoping that they didn't hear the crash. It seems to have gone unnoticed.

Possibly that's what I mean. She giggles. *How stupid. I can't even remember what it's called. Whatever it was, it made me sleep really quickly.*

I push back against the wall and hide behind a pillar as the guards patrol in front of me, moving to the next section. When I can't hear their footsteps anymore, I stick my head around the corner to check that all is clear. Only one of the guards is going in the opposite direction, but his back is toward us.

After calling back softly, "Clear," I tiptoe through the corridor and cringe as the walls vibrate behind me. "Can you step any lighter? You're making the whole floor tremble."

Are you serious? I thought I was super light.

"Yes, I'm serious. You could get us busted."

I cast a glance over my shoulder at the guard going in the opposite direction. He halts and starts to turn. Scooting backward, I press myself up against the wall, hoping that he won't see my slight form or that he will think that it is part of the pillars. I suck in a breath and hold it as his eyes scan the area. The few seconds he studies the corridor feels like hours. Finally, he turns, and I let my breath escape.

That was close, Elan's voice echoes in my head.

I jump, holding a hand over my heart. I'm not keen to answer her in case my whispers echo in the corridor.

A light shines in the distance, and I quicken my pace until I spot the entrance. Two guards stand on patrol outside the open door. I turn to Elan and indicate for her to go out the door.

Do you want me to go ahead without you? she asks, sounding surprised.

I nod. She will be able to leave without being noticed while she's invisible. I stand on my tiptoes and pace in front of her then look at where I think she is.

Yeah, yeah. I get it. Walk quietly.

I bob my head up and down enthusiastically.

The ground still shakes slightly as the dragon paces to the door. Stealthily, I continue forward, keeping an eye on the guards and their reactions and doing my best to stay out of sight. Something grabs a guard's attention, and he moves slightly from his spot, searching the area. Elan must be outside by now, and I'm guessing that the rumble of her footsteps or something similar must have alerted him.

I pause and look for something to use for a distraction, but the palace floor is spotless, and

I curse silently. Quickly, I search my pockets, and I almost cheer when my hand grasps the keys to the dragon stall. I thought I left them in the cell. I fling them in the opposite direction of the entrance, and they clatter against the marble floor. Instantly, both guards spin to look, and they trot off in that direction to investigate. Using this opportunity, I sneak past and out the door then duck around the palace corner, out of sight, before they return. I pant heavily, happy that my plan worked.

Something brushes against my skin. I jump and spin around to see nothing.

It's all right. It's just me. Elan's voice pierces my thoughts, and I breathe a sigh of relief.

"Oh, thank Vanir!"

Jump on my back, and let's get out of here.

"Um. That's a good idea, except I can't see you."

She giggles. *Of course. Here.*

Her golden form appears in front of me, and I climb on, grabbing on to her neck tightly. "I think I'm going to have to make a saddle or something so that I can hang on to you better. Your scales can get quite slippery at times."

She turns invisible and pushes off the ground, and my hands slip. Quickly, I dive forward and embrace her neck. "Not to mention, it's challenging to grab on to you properly when I can't see what I'm grabbing."

Then a saddle is probably a good idea, she says.

"Where are you taking me?"

I'm taking you back to the academy. Then they won't know that you were missing and that you're the one who broke me out of the palace.

"Actually, can you take me to the dragon stalls instead? I need you to talk with the brown dragon that was injured. Hildr is trying to make friends, and so far, I don't think she's succeeding. Although she seems to be able to get a bit closer when she wants to put the ointment on his wound."

Do you mean Drogon?

"I don't know. He hasn't told us his name because he was too hurt and angry over his leg. But he is much more receptive than a lot of the older dragons."

Yup, sounds like Drogon. He is actually really nice. He hasn't been attacked too much, but he is a little bit bitter toward Valkyries of the winged kind. But I have hope for him. Let's go and chat with him. She veers around and heads straight to the dragon stalls.

When we get there, she lands on the cliff entrance of Drogon's stall. Instantly, I spot Hildr closer to the dragon and talking with him, and Eir is standing not far away.

Eir spins around, eyes wide, searching for what caused the noise at the entrance of the cave. Her shoulders relax when she sees me sitting in midair.

Drogon stands upright and Hildr peers at him, looking confused. "What's wrong with you?"

Elan turns visible. *It shows that he knows I'm here. That's all. Stand at ease, Drogon. It's just me, not my mother.*

The young dragon relaxes his shoulders and looks down at Hildr.

Elan is looking at the dragon. Her head is moving, and her eyes are twitching, and the brown dragon is responding likewise. I assume that they are having a private conversation.

Drogon looks at Hildr then back at Elan. It takes a moment before resignation and acceptance flash through the dragon's eyes.

Elan turns to me. *Can you remove his shackles? He promises to be good. And to remain here despite the fact that he hates the enclosure and being a captive. I said if he stays and cooperates, he will be treated well by Hildr.*

"Of course he will!" Hildr almost yells.

Elan tilts her head at Hildr in acknowledgment. *He has agreed, for now. He also said that if you can remove his shackles, Hildr can climb on his back. Despite his leg hurting, he can fly.*

Hildr stands, her eyes full of enthusiasm and excitement. "Really?"

Elan's teeth show in a threatening display that I have learned means a smile. *Yes, really.*

Hildr thrusts her hands into her leather pockets and pulls out a skeleton key and sets to work on his chains. After a few seconds of fiddling with the lock, it pops open, freeing Drogon. And true to Elan's words, Drogon folds his front legs so that he is low enough for Hildr to climb on.

Without a moment's hesitation, Hildr climbs on, throws a hand around his neck, and clasps onto his scales, ducking to avoid the spikes protruding from his head and upper neck.

"Hang on tight, Hildr!" I call as Drogon pushes off into the air.

- CHAPTER TEN -

Hildr takes off on Drogon, and I clench my teeth when he flops sideways, weaving unsteadily all over the place. Eir moves to stand next to me, just in time to see Hildr flick to the side with one of the jerky movements of the dragon. Only her arms being secured tightly around his neck stops her from falling to her death.

Eir gasps loudly, and my teeth clench tighter. We can't do anything for her other than hope that she manages to stay on the dragon's back. The dragon peers over his shoulder, sees what is happening, and jolts around to try to catch her on his back again. It takes several nail-biting attempts with Hildr flicking from one side to the other. Her arms wrapped around the dragon's neck is her only stability. Eventually, one of the flicks flings her body the right distance so that she can hook a leg over his side and dig her heels into the dragon's ribs again.

"That was close." Eir continues to watch the progression with a horrified expression.

"Yes, it was."

It's okay. I know he can look after her like I looked after you. You should organize those saddles though.

Hildr and the dragon become more synchronized with each circuit they execute over the area. Strange pride fills my chest, and I have more hope for the future between dragons and Valkyries.

"It looks like a perfect match." Awe radiates in Eir's voice. "Hildr seems completely satisfied with this one. I think they will work it out and get along well."

"If that's the case, then that's two of us joined with dragons. Perhaps we can slowly build this up into a private army. One to fight against the alliance that is enslaving the dragons and also to fight against the discrimination against the wingless Valkyries and help protect the future of Asgard."

Elan looks down at me. Her mouth is broad, and her teeth show. It's that scary smile again. *That sounds like a plan. Except I don't think Mother will give over any more dragons. We will have to do it ourselves.*

"Do I get a dragon?" Eir asks, a hopeful expression in her eyes.

"As far as I remember, only one more friendly dragon is in this enclosure. And that's the simple dragon. Naga's not the brightest, but he has a sweet personality."

Eir's eyes light up. She clasps her hands together and bobs up and down excitedly. "I love him! He's so cute! I will certainly give him a go."

Then it sounds like you will have a dragon, Elan says.

"He has a kind heart, just like you. You should be a perfect match."

She jumps up and down with excitement. "I can't wait! Actually, I'm going to check on him now."

I'm about to say something when she cuts me off. "Don't worry. I'll avoid his sneezes." She spins to leave then halts.

"What's wrong?" I turn to look when something catches my eye—a soldier.

"Sire," he calls.

Eir turns to face me, a horrified expression on her face. A second later, my expression imitates hers.

Odin's bulk has filled out the entrance to the dragon's pen. He points at me. "Seize her! And capture that dragon."

I jerk Eir's arm and climb on Elan's back. "Come, Eir. It's time to get out of here."

She jumps on Elan's back and loops her arms around my waist as I lean forward and clasp mine around Elan's neck and secure my hands on her scales. Then Elan pushes off into the sky while turning invisible. I don't know what the plan is, but I'm not willing to be seized by Odin at this moment. I am pretty sure he has worked out what I've done.

The End

ACKNOWLEDGMENTS

I am touched by the enormous amount of support I have received from my immediate family. My husband has been a helpful first reader and at times been a wonderful motivator, with hints of ideas to help me through the blanks. The support from my three sons has also been overwhelming. They have put up with my head being in the clouds, thinking about the next plot twist or story for several years. Along with many hours spent working on my books and keeping in touch with my readers.

A big thank you to my extended family who support me being a book enthusiast.

A huge thank you to my editor, Susannah Driver, her editing and writing tips, and my Proofreader, Jessie B, for picking up the things we missed.

Thank you to all of my readers who have loved my work, and continue to read my stories. I would love for you to share your thoughts in a review on one or all of the following:

Amazon.com

Goodreads

Barnes & Noble

You can follow Katrina Cope at:

https://www.facebook.com/Author.Katrina.Cope

https://twitter.com/Katrina_R_Cope

https://www.goodreads.com/author/show/7265107.Katrina_Cope

https://www.katrinacopebooks.com

http://http://www.amazon.com/Katrina-Cope/e/B00F00JF9M/

Book 3 of Valkyrie Academy Dragon Alliance Series 'Scorned' released September 2019.

BOOKS BY KATRINA COPE

~~~~~

Pre-Teen Books

THE SANCTUM SERIES

JAYDEN'S CYBERMOUNTAIN

SCARLET'S ESCAPE

TAYLOR'S PLIGHT

ERIC & THE BLACK AXES

ADRIANNA'S SURGE

~~~~~

Young Adult Urban Fantasy

AFTERLIFE SERIES

FLEDGLING

THE TAKING

ANGELIC RETRIBUTION

DIVIDED PATHS

Afterlife Novelette

THE GATEKEEPER

~~~~~

Young Adult Urban Paranormal Fantasy

SUPERNATURAL EVOLVEMENT SERIES

(Associated with the Afterlife Series)

WITCH'S LEGACY (#0.5 Prequel)

AALIYAH

~~~~~

Young Adult Fantasy Nordic Myths

VALKYRIE ACADEMY DRAGON ALLIANCE

SERIES

MARKED (Prequel)

CHOSEN

VANISHED

SCORNED

INFLICTED

EMPOWERED

GET UPDATES & NOTIFICATIONS OF GIVEAWAYS

Would you like a FREE copy of Marked?
Visit here:
https://www.katrinacopebooks.com/valkyrie-academy-dragon-alliance

Through this link you can sign up for my newsletter and receive a FREE copy of Marked plus updates about my fantasy books, sales and notification of giveaways.

DID YOU ENJOY THIS BOOK?
YOU CAN MAKE A BIG DIFFERENCE.

Honest reviews of my books help bring them to the attention of other readers.

If you've enjoyed this book, I'd be grateful if you could spend a few minutes leaving a review (it can be as short as you like).
The review can be left on Amazon and Goodreads.
Thank you very much.

ABOUT THE AUTHOR

Katrina is an author of several Young Adult and Preteen/Middle Grade novels. Each of her released books reaching the top 100 in certain categories on the Amazon's Best Sellers Rank – a few even as high as number one.

She resides in Queensland, Australia. Her three teenage boys and husband for over nineteen years treat her like a princess. Unfortunately though, this princess still has to do domestic chores.

From a very young age, she has been a very creative person and has spent many years travelling the world and observing many different personalities and cultures. Her favourite personalities have been the strange ones, yet the ones under the radar also hold a place in her heart.

During her last extensive travels, she spent 16 nights in a bomb shelter on a Kibbutz 8 kilometers off the Lebanese border. It was to avoid Katyusha bombs that the resident volunteers decided to name her after (she is still trying to work out why).

Katrina's online home is at
www.katrinacopebooks.com

You can connect with Katrina on:

Twitter https://twitter.com/Katrina_R_Cope

Facebook
https://www.facebook.com/Author.Katrina.Cope

Instagram
https://www.instagram.com/katrina_cope_author

Pinterest
https://www.pinterest.com.au/katrinacope56

Email authorkatrinacope@gmail.com